# TEXAS LONGHORNS

BY K.C. KELLEY

Published by The Child's World®
1980 Lookout Drive • Mankato, MN 56003-1705
800-599-READ • www.childsworld.com

Copyright ©2022 by The Child's World®
All rights reserved. No part of this book may be reproduced or utilized in any form or by any means without written permission from the publisher.

Cover: Nick Wagner/Austin American-Statesman/AP Images.
Interior: AP Images: Sam C. Pierson Jr./Houston Chronicle 8; Paul Sakuma 11; Tim Sharp 19. Dreamstime: Noamfein 4; Bingram 12 top; Ecoimagesphotos 12 bottom top. Newscom: John Rivera/Icon Sportswire 15; Louis DeLuca/MCT; Dennis Hubbard/Icon SMI. Wikimedia: 7 (2).

Thanks to Conor Buckley for his help with this book.

ISBN 9781503850408 (Reinforced Library Binding)
ISBN 9781503850651 (Portable Document Format)
ISBN 9781503851412 (Online Multi-user eBook)
LCCN: 2021930298

Printed in the United States of America

*Texas players celebrate another great play for the Longhorns.*

# CONTENTS

Why We Love College Football   4

CHAPTER ONE
## Early Days   6

CHAPTER TWO
## Glory Years   9

CHAPTER THREE
## Best Year Ever!   10

CHAPTER FOUR
## Texas Traditions   13

CHAPTER FIVE
## Meet the Mascot   14

CHAPTER SIX
## Top Texas QBs   17

CHAPTER SEVEN
## Other Texas Heroes   18

CHAPTER EIGHT
## Recent Superstars   21

Glossary   22

Find Out More   23

Index   24

# WHY WE LOVE COLLEGE FOOTBALL

The leaves are changing color. Happy crowds fill the stadiums. Pennants wave. And here come the fight songs. It's time for college football! The sport is one of America's most popular. Millions of fans follow their favorite teams. They wear school colors and hope for big wins.

*Fans wearing the Texas "burnt orange" color fill the stadium for another big game!*

The Texas Longhorns have a long history of winning football games. The team has more than 900 wins! Texas has won many championships and trophies. Fans always love to "Hook 'em Horns!"

CHAPTER ONE

# Early Days

The Texas Longhorns first played football in 1893. They had just four games that year. They shut out their opponents in each one! After the season they were named the "best team in Texas!"

In 1894, two of the Longhorns' biggest **rivalries** began. They beat Texas A&M and Arkansas that year. In 1900, they started another great rivalry. Texas beat the University of Oklahoma 28–2.

**TIME OUT!**
The first football game for Texas had to take a time out. The ball popped! A fan rode a horse to town to get a new football.

The early 1900s was a great time for Texas football. They were **undefeated** four times from 1900 to 1920. They had a **winning record** every year but one from 1902 to 1933.

*Above: Look how much rounder the 1893 football was in this Texas team photo.*

*Right: The 1915 team was one of the highest scoring schools in the nation.*

CHAPTER TWO

# Glory Years

In the 1940s, Texas was one of the country's best teams. In 1941, the team was featured on the cover of *Life* magazine. That was the first year the Longhorns were ranked number one. They won three Southwest **Conference** titles in the decade.

Coach Darrell Royal took over in 1957. He led the team to its first national championship in 1963. With Royal as coach, the Longhorns won the title again in 1969 and 1970. During Royal's time at Texas, the Longhorns never had a losing record! He was the best Texas coach ever.

**BIG GAME**
Texas won the national title in 1969. They earned it by winning a famous game over Arkansas. The Longhorns trailed by 14 points. Then they rallied to score a late touchdown. Texas won "the game of the century" 15–14.

― *Left: On the way to a national title, Jim Bertelsen scored on this play late in a win over Arkansas.*

## CHAPTER THREE

# Best Year Ever!

The 2005 season was the Longhorns' best. They began ranked number two. The team then won 12 games in a row. That put them into the national championship game. They faced **defending champion** USC. Some experts said the Trojans were the best team ever. Texas quarterback Vince Young thought differently. He ran for 200 yards and three touchdowns. The third score came on the Longhorns' last play. Young ran to the right and jumped into the end zone! Texas won 41–38. They were crowned the national champions!

*Vince Young heads for the end zone to give Texas the winning points in their big showdown with USC.*

# LONGHORNS

*Above:* Shown after a big win, the Texas Tower stands 307 feet tall.

*Below:* Students quickly learn to make the "Hook 'em Horns" sign with their hand.

CHAPTER FOUR

# Texas Traditions

The Texas Longhorns have a long history with many great traditions. One is very tall . . . and very colorful! The University of Texas tower stands in the middle of **campus**. The tower lights up orange when the Longhorns win! If the team wins the national title, the tower's lights form a big number **1**.

One of the most famous Texas traditions is their hand sign. It is called "Hook 'em Horns." The signal began in 1955. Fans hold their pinkie and pointer fingers so they look like the horns of a longhorn cow!

**BIG RIVALRY**

The Red River Showdown is one of college football's biggest rivalries. Texas plays Oklahoma. The rivalry began in 1900. That was before Oklahoma was officially a state!

## CHAPTER FIVE

# Meet the Mascot

A Texas longhorn is a special kind of cow. It is known for its huge horns. The biggest horns on one of these cows measured 10 feet (3 meters) from tip to tip! Longhorns found in Texas came from cattle brought by Spanish **colonists**. The colors of the animals inspired the colors of the team. Texas wears burnt orange and white like a longhorn's hair.

The Texas mascot is a real longhorn named Bevo. The team has been using a live mascot since 1916. There have been 15 different longhorns named Bevo. He shows up to cheer on the team at home games.

### HOME FIELD
Since 1924, the Longhorns have played in Texas Memorial Stadium. The stadium is huge. It can fit 100,119 screaming fans! The stadium has the first **HD video screen** ever put in a college stadium. The huge screen is nicknamed "Godzillatron."

*Students are trained to bring Bevo onto the field. They also take care of Bevo when he's not working at games.*

14

CHAPTER SIX

# Top Texas QBs

Bobby Layne was the QB for great Texas teams in the 1940s. Layne was named to the All-Conference team four times. He won 28 games as the **starting** QB.

Vince Young played for the team from 2003 to 2005. His quick feet and fast running made him a star. He leads all Texas players with an **average** of 6.8 yards per carry. He helped win the national championship in 2005.

Colt McCoy picked up where Young left off. This superstar led the Longhorns from 2006 to 2009. He has more wins than any other quarterback in the school's history. His overall record was 45–8.

— *Left: Colt McCoy threw 112 touchdown passes for the Longhorns. That is still the most in school history!*

## CHAPTER SEVEN

# Other Texas Heroes

The Heisman Trophy is college football's highest honor. Two Texas players have won it.

In 1977, running back Earl Campbell was the first. He was nicknamed "The Tyler Rose" after his Texas hometown. In four seasons, he ran for 4,443 yards and 40 touchdowns. He later made it to the Pro Football Hall of Fame.

Ricky Williams played for the Longhorns from 1995 to 1998. He won the team's second Heisman trophy in 1998. Ricky Williams was an all-around athlete. He was drafted by pro baseball's Philadelphia Phillies after high school. He stuck with football and became a Longhorns legend.

*Ricky Williams ran for an amazing 2,124 yards in 1998. He scored 27 touchdowns as well. No wonder he won the Heisman!*

CHAPTER EIGHT

# Recent Superstars

**Linebacker** Derrick Johnson was a three-time member of the **All-America** team. In 2004, he won the Bronko Nagurski Award. That goes to the nation's top defensive player.

Another great Texas linebacker was Brian Orakpo. His best year came in 2008 when he was named as an All-America team member. Orakpo played 10 NFL seasons for Washington and Tennessee.

### BIG LEG
**Punters** are not usually big stars. But Texas had one of the best ever. Born in Australia, Michael Dickson began at Texas in 2015. In 2017, he won the Ray Guy award for best punter. Dickson has become a star in the NFL for Seattle.

Jordan Shipley won the 2009 Paul Warfield trophy. That goes to the country's best receiver. Shipley was also a great kick returner. In the 2008 Red River Showdown he scored on 96-yard return to help the Longhorns win.

*Left: Here's Brian Orakpo doing what he did best for Texas—blasting past blockers and aiming for the quarterback!*

21

# GLOSSARY

**All-America** (ALL uh-MAYR-ih-kuh) an honor given to the top players in college sports

**campus** (KAM-puss) the grounds and buildings of a school.

**colonists** (KALL-uh-nists) people who settle a land not their own.

**conference** (KON-fur-enss) a group of schools that play sports against each other.

**defending champion** (deh-FEN-ding CHAMP-ee-un) the team that won the previous season.

**HD video** (H-D VID-ee-oh) high-definition video; a very sharp way to show moving pictures.

**rivalries** (RYE-vul-reez) teams that play each other year after year.

**starting** (START-ing) in sports, team members that play at the beginning of a game.

**undefeated** (un-deh-FEE-ted) not beaten in a series of games.

**winning record** (WIN-ning REK-urd) when a team wins more games than it loses.

## FIND OUT MORE

### IN THE LIBRARY

Holmes, Parker. *Texas vs. Oklahoma.*
New York, NY: PowerKids Press, 2013.

Sports Illustrated Kids. *The Greatest Teams of All Time.* New York, NY: Sports Illustrated Kids, 2018.

Stewart, Mark. *The Texas Longhorns.*
Chicago, IL: Norwood House Press, 2010.

Temple, Ramey. *Texas Longhorns.*
New York, NY: AV2 by Weigl, 2020.

### ON THE WEB

Visit our website for links about the
**Texas Longhorns**:
**childsworld.com/links**

Note to Parents, Teachers, and Librarians: We routinely verify our Web links to make sure they are safe and active sites. So encourage your readers to check them out!

# INDEX

Arkansas 6, 9
Bertelsen, Jim 9
Bevo 14
Campbell, Earl 18
Godzillatron 14
Heisman Trophy 18
"Hook 'em, Horns!" 5, 12, 13
Johnson, Derrick 21
Layne, Bobby 17
McCoy, Colt 17
Nagurski Award 21
Oklahoma 6, 13
Orakpo, Brian 21

Philadelphia Phillies 18
Red River Showdown 13, 21
Royal, Darrell 9
Shipley, Jordan 21
Southwest Conference 9
Texas A&M 6
Texas Memorial Stadium 14
USC Trojans 10
Warfield trophy 21
Williams, Ricky 18
Young, Vince 10, 17

# ABOUT THE AUTHOR

**K.C. Kelley** is the author of more than 100 sports books for young readers, including numerous biographies of famous athletes. He went to the University of California—Berkeley, but his Golden Bears didn't quite make it into this series!